ROCK U.S.A. ™
and...
The American Way!

Written by Edna Cucksey Stephens
Illustrated by Mark J. Herrick

For my husband, Mark, and my children, Scot and Cari, for their love and continued support as I pursue my American Dream,
and
For all the teachers in our great country.

E.C.S.

I give thanks for the opportunity of working on this book to my friend, Edna, who has the vision to
see the need for helping children learn our American values and to God for the power of love to produce the work.
I dedicate this book to my parents, my godson, Austin William Bryan Smith, to my friends and to all the kids of the world.

M.J.H.

Special thanks to the wonderful people at
EDCO Publishing
and
Mitchell Graphics
who always give their personal best.

A portion of the proceeds from this book will benefit the September 11th Families of Freedom Scholarship Fund™.

Katharine Lee Bates wrote the first version of America The Beautiful in 1893. She wrote the version we know today in 1913.

America

As American as Apple pie...
Thank you,
Johnny Appleseed!

Made up of fifty *united states* and people from many different backgrounds, America has been called the *land of opportunity* and the *land of liberty*. In America, all people can enjoy the many blessings of freedom!

Allegiance...

We show patriotism and loyalty to our country by saying the *Pledge of Allegiance* to the flag...

I pledge allegiance to the flag of the United States of America and to the Republic for which it stands, one nation, under God, indivisible, with liberty and justice for all.

Meet two very patriotic ants!

Antonio Ant   Abigail Ant

American Red Cross

This volunteer organization was founded on May 21, 1881, in Washington, D.C., by Clara Barton. She served as a volunteer nurse during the American Civil War and saw the need for a Red Cross society in the United States. Under her leadership, the American Red Cross became the number one disaster relief organization in the world and remains so today.

Reddy Freddy is a helper in times of need! You can be helpful, too!

Hawaii

ALASKA

E PLURI

E Pluribus Unum... *is latin and means -*

out of many, one. You will find this motto on the Great Seal of the United States. It refers to the creation of one nation from 13 colonies. Today, America is made up of 50 unique states. The citizens of the United States come from many *different* cultures and practice many *different* traditions and religions, but *ALL are united* under one government and *ALL* are Americans.

(Look at some coins and a dollar bill. See if you can find the motto *E PLURIBUS UNUM*.)

ple pie is an American tradition!

LAND OF THE FREE...
HOME OF THE BRAVE...
FROM SEA TO SHINING SEA...
THERE'S <u>NO</u> BETTER
PLACE TO BE!

ROCK U.S.A.™ reminds us to be
PROUD to be an AMERICAN...
EVERYDAY!

E PLURIBUS UNUM

The
American Dream
means different things to
different people. In America,
each person has the freedom
to choose and pursue his or her
individual
American Dream.

"My *American Dream*
is to be a famous
Artist."

Henry Ford founded the
Ford Motor Company in 1903. His new
method of mass production made cars
affordable for people across America.
Ford's assembly line factories and higher wages
brought workers to Michigan from all over
the country. As more and more
automobile factories
opened, people
everywhere began
calling Detroit the
"Motor City."

"This *ANT*ique
car is really
COOL!"

Automobiles

Automobiles are important in the daily lives
of most Americans. They take us to work, to school and to play.
Automobiles help us travel to see and enjoy the diverse beauty
and many scenic places found across our great country.
   Automobiles are also important American products.
The automotive industry has been important in America's history.
Today, it continues to provide jobs for many people in America
and is important to our country's economy.

1909 Model T Ford
Runabout

The American bald eagle was adopted as the national bird on June 20, 1782. It represents courage, independence and strength.

Bill of Rights
THIRD CHARTER OF FREEDOM

1

Legislative Branch

The Bill of Rights

Some of the delegates who wrote the Constitution in 1787 later felt more rights should be added to the Constitution to protect people against government. In 1791, they added ten *amendments*. These first ten amendments are known as the Bill of Rights. The Bill of Rights is one of three documents called the Charters of Freedom. The Declaration of Independence and the Constitution are the other two. The 462 words in the Bill of Rights list ten promises that protect the rights of *all Americans.*

THE FIRST TEN AMENDMENTS...

First: Freedom of religion, speech, press, assembly and petition
Second: Right to bear arms
Third: Limited quartering of soldiers in citizens' homes
Fourth: Regulated searches and seizures
Fifth: Right to due process of law, including protection
     against self-incrimination
Sixth: Rights of a person accused of a crime, right to an attorney
Seventh: Right to trial by jury
Eighth: Forbids unfair bail, fines and punishment
Ninth: Entitles citizens to rights not listed in the Constitution
Tenth: Powers not listed are reserved to the states or the people

Today the Constitution has 27 amendments.

Boston Tea Party

Become a Baseball player!

The BOSTON
TEA PARTY

On December 16, 1773, to protest a tax on tea, a group of patriots (colonists who wanted *independence* for the American colonies) dressed as Native Americans and boarded a British ship. They dumped tons of tea into Boston harbor. They also boycotted (refused to buy) English products to protest the high taxes. The colonists no longer wanted to be ruled by the English King and Parliament. They wanted their independence, their own country and the right to make their own laws!

2
Executive Branch

3
Judicial Branch

BRANCHES OF Government

The delegates who helped write and approve the Constitution wanted to make sure that the United States would never be ruled by just one person or group. To keep this from happening, they decided that the powers of government should be divided. This idea is known as the *separation of powers*.

Articles I, II and III of the Constitution divides the powers of our government into *three branches*.

I. *Legislative Branch* - made up of Congress (the Senate and the House of Representatives). This branch has the power to:
- Make laws
- Print and coin money
- Provide for and maintain the armed forces

II. *Executive Branch* - made up of the President. This branch:
- Makes sure the laws are carried out
- Heads the armed forces
- Appoints citizens to government positions
- Makes treaties
- Signs or vetoes laws

III. *Judicial Branch* - made up of the Supreme Court and other national courts. This branch:
- Explains the meaning of laws
- Decides whether laws passed by Congress can be related back to laws provided for in the Constitution

United States

New York, on
d seven hundred and eightynine.

Writing the Bill of Rights was the right thing to do for our country and its citizens!

INK

ROCK U.S.A.

How a "Bill" Becomes a Law!

National laws are made in Congress.

Congress is made up of *two houses* or *groups*, the Senate and the House of Representatives. Each *new law* first begins as someone's idea. The idea is then written as a bill. A bill may begin in either the Senate or the House of Representatives. First, a Standing Committee (a small group of legislators who studies and reports on bills) looks over the bill and does one of three things:

  1. sends the bill back with no changes   2. makes changes and sends it back   3. tables the bill (does nothing with it).
If the committee sends the bill back with no changes, then the bill goes on the calendar to be voted on.
In the Senate over half the Senators (51 of 100) must vote yes and in the House over half of the Representatives (218 of 435) must <u>vote yes</u> to <u>pass the bill</u>. If the bill passes it moves to the other branch of Congress.
If the bill is passed in both the House and the Senate, it then goes to the President to be signed into law.
If the President *vetoes* the bill, it can still become a law if two-thirds of both the Senate and House vote in favor of it.

United States Constitution

· 1787 ·

"The Constitution will continue to live and grow as long as people believe in democracy and cherish freedom!"

At the Constitutional Convention held in Philadelphia, delegates from the 13 original states (colonies) wrote down the laws of the land in the Constitution. It was approved by 39 delegates from 12 states on September 15, 1787. Rhode Island did not send any delegates.

George Washington was the most important man there. He was chosen to serve as president of the convention and was the first to sign the Constitution.

James Madison of Virginia, known as the *father of the Constitution* was the only delegate to take notes during the convention. His notes are the only record of what went on during the convention.

Ben Franklin has been called the wise man of the convention. He was a delegate from Pennsylvania. At 81, he was the oldest of the 55 delegates.

The Constitution has served as a model for many countries around the world. It is the main guide or outline for governing our country.

Building America's future!

BE A CARPENTER!

<u>Words from the Preamble</u> (introduction that explains its purpose) to the Constitution: *"We, the people of the United States, in order to form a more perfect Union... establish this Constitution for the United States of America."*

CHILDREN ARE THE FUTURE

Providing a quality education and assuring the well-being of *ALL* children is the *key to the future* of America.
"Patriotism is not so much protecting the land of our fathers as preserving the land of our children."

Jose Ortega Y Gasset

Children are

Capitol of the United States of America

In 1790 William Thornton, a doctor and amateur architect, won the contest to design the Capitol Building. His prize was $500 and a city lot.

Congress makes laws in the Capitol.

Nice work, guys! The Constitution is our nation's *most important* document!

WOW! The Constitution was written over 200 years ago!

Yes, Abby, and it still works today. Our *Founding Fathers* were *really* smart!

The U.S. Constitution...

gives the power of making national laws to the legislative branch of our government which is the U.S. Congress. Congress is made up of two "houses" or groups, the Senate and the House of Representatives. Senators and Representatives are elected by the people of their states. *Representatives* serve two-year terms. *Senators* serve six-year terms.

the future!

The Capitol of the United States is located in Washington, D.C. Congress has met here for over 200 years to make our national laws. The U.S. Capitol is a *symbol* of Congress and our democratic government. The cornerstone of the Capitol was laid by George Washington in 1793.

The Capitol's dome is a famous symbol of our country. The Capitol does not have a front and back door. Instead, we say it has an east front and a west front. Most visitors enter from the east front.

The Capitol has two chambers (large meeting rooms). The House of Representatives meets in the chamber on the south side of the Capitol. The 435 Representatives sit on benches and do not have assigned seats.

The Senate meets in a chamber on the north side of the Capitol. Each of the 100 Senators has a special assigned seat. The Republicans sit on one side and the Democrats on the other.

Only a few members of Congress have an office in the Capitol. Most members of Congress have offices in nearby buildings.

Declaration of
Adopted July 4, 1776

The name United States of America first appeared officially in the Declaration of Independence.

The Declaration of Independence outlines the rights of the people, summarizes a list of abuses committed by King George III of England against the American colonists and declares them to be free and independent.

Thomas Jefferson wrote most of the Declaration of Independence. It took him about two weeks to write it. Ben Franklin and John Adams made some changes to his first draft. The document was then presented to the members of the Second Continental Congress and they made a few more changes.

John Hancock was the president of the Congress. He signed the draft of the Declaration on July 4, 1776. After New York approved it on July 15th, it was certified by Charles Thomson, secretary of the Congress. The document was then hand-printed on parchment, and signed by 50 delegates on August 2nd. Later, six more members of the Congress signed the document making a total of 56 signers.

The Declaration of Independence is on display along with the Constitution and the Bill of Rights, at the National Archives building in Washington, D.C.

Tony, this is a very import*ANT* *quill* pen!

Right, Abby! I hope there is enough ink for *John Hancock!*

The four parts of the Declaration of Independence...

1. The *preamble,* or introduction, sets forth the objectives. It begins with the words, "When in the course of human events..."

2. The *declaration of rights* of the people. "...all men are created equal... with certain... Rights... among these Life, Liberty and the pursuit of Happiness."

3. A *list of complaints...* against King *George III.*

4. A *pledge by the signers* of their Lives, Fortunes and their sacred Honor in the cause of freedom.

Independence

Care for and teach people how to stay healthy!

Be a Doctor!

The *signers* were brave men who took great risks in the name of *freedom*!

The 56 signers

of the Declaration of Independence were very brave men. They pledged their lives, fortunes and sacred honor to the cause of independence and freedom.

Signing the Declaration was a very *dangerous* thing to do. If the American colonists had not won the Revolutionary War, the signers could have been *shot for treason*.

John Hancock signed his name in very large letters. He wanted to be sure that King George III could read his signature without his glasses.

Diversity helps make our country great! Except for Native Americans, the United States is a nation of people who left their home countries looking for a better life. For this reason, the United States is sometimes called the *"melting pot."*

Today the population of the United States is made up of people from many different countries, with different customs, traditions and beliefs. Americans are a diverse people with many different likes, dislikes, talents and dreams! But even though we are all different, <u>*we are all Americans*</u>.

★ Diversity ★

Thomas Jefferson and John Adams died on the same day, July 4, 1826, exactly 50 years after the Declaration of Independence was approved.

Today, there are a total of *538 electoral votes*. This number is equal to the total number of members of Congress.

Each state is given a specific number of *electoral votes.*
This number is equal to the number of members it has in the United States Congress.

The Electoral College

The Electoral College was set up by the Constitution more than 200 years ago. The Founding Fathers wanted a fair way to choose a president and vice president for our country. They had a hard time deciding how this should be done. They agreed on the Electoral College method.

This *"college"* is not a place. It is a group that meets to complete a special duty. This special duty is to elect the President of the United States.

The electoral votes are based on how the people in each state voted.

The winning party ticket in each state wins all the electoral votes in that state.

The political party in each state chooses its electors. They meet in December, after the election, in their state capitals to cast their votes.

These electoral votes are put into sealed envelopes and sent to the president of the U.S. Senate. On January 6, he opens the envelopes and reads the results in a meeting of the entire U.S. Congress. If there is a tie, or if no one gets a majority of the votes, the House of Representatives must decide who will be president. *Each state has only one vote.* A tie in the number of electoral votes has only happened two times in our country's history.

Quality *schools* plus
well-prepared *teachers*
equal
Grade A Citizens!

"Ooh...
ooh, baby,
Ant America grand?"

Be ant... Entertainer

Write a song and sing about living in America.

Our Founding Fathers knew the importance of education. In 1787, the year the Constitution was ratified, John Adams said, *"Children should be educated and instructed in the principles of freedom."*

ollege

Eagle

The bald Eagle is a living symbol of the United States. It is found only in North America and stands for strength and bravery. In 1782, Congress chose to put the bald eagle on the Great Seal which is the official stamp or mark of the United States.

Ellis Island

Located in New York City's harbor, directly across from the island of Manhattan.

In the early years of our country there were no national immigration laws. Each state controlled immigration inside its borders. In 1891, the federal government established the office of Superintendent of Immigration. The next year, Ellis Island was opened and was used as an immigration station. It was in operation from 1892 to 1954. During these 62 years, more than 12 million immigrants passed through its doors looking for freedom and a better life. To all of them, Ellis Island was the *island of hope*.

I'm a
LIFE-LONG LEARNER!
I know there is still a LOT
I need to know!

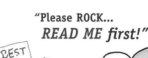

"You have to read and learn a lot to be an Astron*ANT* like me!"

Education

Americans understand the importance of a quality education.
Knowledge is power.
Education opens doors to unlimited opportunities and provides the skills to be successful, productive citizens. Educating America's children is the key to a strong democracy *now... and for the future.*

"Please ROCK...
READ ME first!"

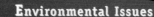

Flag OF THE United States

OLD GLORY!

All Americans far and near... fly the flag and hold it dear!

For most people, the flag represents our national heritage. This is why we pay special honor to *"Old Glory"* on Flag Day.

In 1777, a committee headed by George Washington designed a flag. Betsy Ross probably made the first flag following George Washington's instructions. Without a doubt, she is responsible for the idea of a five-pointed star. The thirteen stars in this flag were arranged in a circle and stood for the 13 colonies.

On June 14, 1777, the Continental Congress proclaimed that *"the Flag of the United States be 13 stripes alternate red and white, and the Union be 13 stars in a blue field..."*

Although there is no known record which explains why the Congress chose red, white and blue for the flag's colors, we know the colors did have meaning when they were chosen for the Great Seal in 1782.

It is written that _red_ is for hardiness and valor, _white_ for purity and innocence and _blue_ for vigilance, and justice. The *stripes* stand for the original 13 colonies and the 50 stars of the current flag represent the 50 states.

Be A... Farmer!

Grow quality food to feed **America** and the world!

FLAG DAY...

was first observed in 1877, on the *centennial* of the flag's adoption. The flag is honored because it is a symbol of our country and all it stands for.

Betsy Ross

The First U.S. Flag

The thirteen stars stand for the original thirteen colonies.

ROCK U.S.A.

AME

FOUNDING FATHERS

These four men and many others were responsible for writing and establishing the Declaration of Independence and Constitution. They were men of vision who wanted to make sure that Americans would always enjoy the *blessings of freedom.*

George Washington was a general in the Revolutionary War. He led Americans in the fight to win freedom from England. He was the first to sign the Constitution. Americans trusted and respected him so much that they elected him to be our *first President.*

John Adams was an outspoken patriot and a leader in the movement for independence. He helped Jefferson draft the Declaration of Independence, was Washington's Vice-President and our country's *second President.*

Thomas Jefferson wrote the Declaration of Independence. He was a lawyer, inventor, an architect and many other things. He served as Governor of his home state of Virginia. In 1800, he was elected our country's *third President.*

Benjamin Franklin was a writer and a printer, discovered electricity, invented bifocals and a stove and organized the postal service. He signed the Declaration of Independence and was the first Governor of Pennsylvania. At the age of 81, he attended the Constitutional Convention and signed the Constitution.

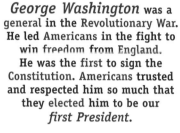

The pledge to the flag is a promise of allegiance to the United States. It was first recited during the National School Celebration held in 1892. In 1942, Congress made the pledge part of the code for the use of the flag.

Some people in the United States, for religious and other reasons, do not pledge their allegiance to the flag. In our country, where freedoms are guaranteed and protected, people have the right to follow their beliefs. But with these many freedoms comes great responsibility.

Our families and friends are the core of our daily lives. They are the fabric of the *American way* of life. Families and friends are the heart of *America.* They are the common thread that connects us and helps us better understand one another.

GREAT SE...

The pyramid stands for long-lasting strength.

The eye and the motto show that the American cause is favored.

The date of the Declaration of Independence is on the base of the pyramid.

On July 4, 1776, just hours after the Declaration of Independence was adopted, Benjamin Franklin, John Adams and Thomas Jefferson were asked to create a seal for the the new nation. Their design was not accepted but the Congress did approve the motto, *"E pluribus unum"* which means, "out of many, one" and stands for one nation that was created from 13 colonies.

The Great Seal was approved six years later on June 20, 1782. It took three committees and 14 people to create a seal that stands for the beliefs and values that the Founding Fathers wanted to pass on to future generations.

In the center of the seal is a bald eagle, our national bird. The 13 stars above the eagle stand for the 13 original states. The stars are surrounded by clouds.

The colors are *red*, which stands for hardiness and valor, *white*, for purity and innocence and *blue*, for vigilance and justice.

A shield with 13 red and white stripes covers the eagle's chest. The stripes represent the 13 original states. The stripes are joined together by a blue band representing the President and Congress.

The olive branch stands for peace. The 13 arrows represent the power of the 13 states and their willingness to fight for freedom.

The reverse side of the Great Seal has a 13-step pyramid with the year 1776 in Roman numerals at the base. At the top of the pyramid is the Eye of Providence.

THE GREAT SE... UNITED STATES

America's unofficial national anthem, *God Bless America,* was composed by an immigrant who left his home in Siberia when he was only five years old. Irving Berlin (1888-1989) wrote the original version of the song during the summer of 1918. He rewrote the song in 1938. Kate Smith introduced it on her radio show on Armistice Day that year. It was an *immediate hit*!

"Good Citizen"

GOD BLESS AMERICA

The GREAT SEAL is our National Coat of Arms.

"The Founding Fathers liked the number...13!"

In the **United States** we have many **opportunities** for **success**.

Give Back!

Giving back is a way to say *"thank you"* for the many blessings of freedom we have in America. We can *give back* by planting a tree, volunteering for a worthy cause, helping a person in need and in many other ways. Remember...

one person **CAN** make a difference!

Y HOME SWEET HOME!

American HEROES

It's all about doing your *personal best*!

Heroes come in many different shapes and sizes. Some are men, some are women, some are alive and some are dead. Some are famous and some are people whose names we do not know. We can read about heroes in history books, but many heroes are people we see every day.

Heroes are positive role models. They are people we admire or people we want to be like. A hero might be the person next door, a teacher, friend, mom, dad, grandma or grandpa. Most heroes do not view themselves as heroes. How they act and what they do is just part of who they are.

Many American heroes died in the military while serving our country.

Many other Americans were heroes on September 11, 2001, the day America was *attacked by terrorists*. We know the names of many of these heroes, but we will never know the exact number of Americans who risked their lives or gave of themselves in ways big and small to make a difference.

We will never forget that day and what it means to all Americans. It also reminds us to be thankful for the heroes in our everyday lives and to be a hero in some small way for others.

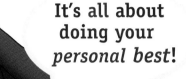

Everyone can be a *hero* to someone, Abby!

Our HEROES

Medal of Honor

OWN A HOME!

To many people owning their <u>own home</u> is a BIG part of their *American Dream!*

The Medal of Honor was established by Abraham Lincoln in 1861. It is the highest award for bravery in action against an enemy force. It can be awarded to any individual serving in the Armed Forces of the United States.

The Medal of Honor is generally presented by the President of the United States in the name of Congress. For this reason, it is often called the Congressional Medal of Honor. It can be given to the next of kin in the name of persons who were killed as a result of their acts of bravery.

Thanks to all American Heroes past and present!

You're _my_ hero, Tony!

Honor Guard

Located in Arlington National Cemetery in Arlington, Virginia.

HERE RESTS IN
HONORED GLORY
AN AMERICAN
SOLDIER
KNOWN BUT TO GOD

Purple Heart

The Purple Heart was created by General George Washington. It is awarded to members of the U.S. armed forces who are wounded in military action. It is given to the next of kin in the name of those who are killed in action or die of wounds received in action. It is also awarded to those wounded or killed as a result of _"an international terrorist attack."_
Purple Heart Medals were awarded to military members or next of kin who were wounded or killed in the terrorist acts of September 11, 2001.

Honor Memorial

The _Tomb of the Unknowns_ honors all the unknown men and women who died fighting for our country and our...
freedom.

The first woman to receive the Purple Heart as a result of combat was First Lt. Annie G. Fox, while serving during the Japanese attack on Pearl Harbor.

Washington was inaugurated on the balcony of Federal Hall on April 30, 1789 in New York City and took the first Presidential oath of office.

Independence
4TH OF JULY

POP! POP!

ZOOOOOM!

BANG!

Late in the afternoon of July 4, 1776, nine of the original 13 colonies voted in favor of issuing a *Declaration of Independence* to King George III of England. The colonists declared their independence and their plans to form a new nation.

Every year since 1776, on the 4th of July, people from all walks of life have come together as Americans to celebrate the birth of our great nation and our *freedom*.

There are big parades and marching bands, flag displays, patriotic songs and lots of fireworks. The fireworks remind us of the words, *"rockets' red glare"* in our <u>national anthem</u>.

The 4th of July is a special day for all Americans when we celebrate our nation, our freedom and our... Founding Fathers!

We're *proud* to be *AmericANTS*!

"That's m favorite song!'

INAUGURATION

Each new President of the United States must take the oath of office. This is done at an inauguration ceremony. The oath begins, *"I do solemnly swear...".*
Every president since George Washington has taken the oath of office. They swear to preserve, protect and defend the Constitution and the laws of the land.

Being President of the United States is a very important job and with the job comes a *huge responsibility*: to safeguard the welfare of the nation.

Writer *Stefan Lorant* referred to the President's job as a *"glorious burden."*

Happy Birthday, America! Keep the spirit *ROCKin!*

POP! POP!

U.S.S. FREEDOM

RAP! RAP! RAP! DISCO!

Be an Iron.. Worker!

Building support systems and strong foundations!

When the colonists heard that the Declaration of Independence had been signed, they built large bonfires and celebrated in the streets.

IMMIGRANTS

In the 62 years between 1892 and 1954, more than 12 million people landed on Ellis Island in New York City's harbor. Most of these people came from Europe and were called *immigrants*. Asian *immigrants* were brought to Angel Island in San Francisco Bay. These men, women and children left their native lands to come to the United States. Some were escaping religious persecution. Others came for better living conditions. Many wanted a better life for their children in the *land of opportunity*. To all of them, America was the *land of hope*. *Immigrants* from many countries still come to America today for these same reasons.

Living in the United States does not automatically mean that one is an American citizen. Residents of the United States can be *aliens*, *nationals* or *citizens*. *Aliens* are people who left a foreign country and came to live in the United States. They have some of the same rights as U.S. citizens, but they cannot vote in elections. *Nationals* are natives of American territories. They have all the legal protections that citizens have, but they do not have the full political rights of U.S. citizens.

Immigrants from other countries who want to become U.S. citizens must apply for and pass a citizenship test. Those who become citizens in this manner are called *naturalized citizens*. Citizens of the United States enjoy all the freedoms, protections and legal rights which the Constitution promises.

Justice For All

Justice for All

is _guaranteed_ by the United States Constitution.
Everyone is _equal_ under the law.

The Articles of the Constitution set up the way our government works. The amendments to the Constitution give us our individual rights. The court system has the job of protecting these rights.

When a problem goes to court, it is either a civil case or a criminal case. In a civil case, someone may feel they were injured wrongly or want to collect money for damages. A criminal case is brought by the government and has penalties that include jail sentences.

Persons accused of a crime have the right to an attorney. If they cannot afford an attorney one will be provided for them by the government. The _prosecutor_ is the lawyer who represents the government and the victims. The _defense attorney_ is the lawyer representing the accused person (_defendant_).

In our country, we have several important laws to remember. The first is that a person is innocent until the evidence proves him or her guilty and the jury agrees. Another rule is that a person must be in the courtroom in order to be tried. A person has to be able to defend himself or herself, but they do not have to speak (Fifth Amendment). The lawyers can only argue about the evidence presented at the trial.

Justice is represented by a blindfolded woman carrying a sword and a scale. She symbolizes fair and equal treatment under the law.

Thomas Jefferson

One of the most well-known of our Founding Fathers, Thomas Jefferson, wrote the Declaration of Independence, was a Secretary of State, Vice President and the third President. He was a man of many talents and interests. Jefferson was also governor of Virginia. During the 83 years of his life, Jefferson was a lawyer, farmer, lawmaker, architect, inventor, archaeologist and musician. He enjoyed studying plants, weather and fossils. He loved books and could read books written in seven languages.

Jefferson spent 50 years building and rebuilding his home. He named it Monticello, and was always thinking of ways to improve it. In 1801, Jefferson authorized the Lewis and Clark Expedition to explore the land between the Mississippi River and the Pacific Ocean.

One of Jefferson's greatest achievements as President was the Louisiana Purchase in 1803. This purchase doubled the size of the nation. This agreement brought Jefferson's dream of a U.S. empire _"from sea to shining sea"_ closer to reality.

Jefferson Memorial

Washington, D.C., is home to this well-known landmark that was built as a memorial to Thomas Jefferson. A 19-foot-high bronze statue of him stands in the middle of a Greek style temple overlooking the Potomac River.

The building that houses the statue honors the Greek and Roman architecture that Jefferson admired. He helped to make these styles popular in the United States.

JURY TRIAL

Order in the Court!

But, Judge! I'm *InnocANT*!

What did he say? ???????? ???????? ????????

Judge ROCK U.S.A.

Your Honor, I'm Art *ANT*eater, the prosecuting *ANT*torney.

I am the Defend*ANT* in this case!

Trial by jury is a right provided for by the U.S. Constitution. In America, a person who is accused of a crime is innocent until proven guilty. When a person is accused of a crime, a trial is held to determine if the person is guilty beyond a reasonable doubt, or innocent. A judge *presides* over the courtroom to maintain order and to make sure that everyone <u>follows the Constitution</u>.

The jury, made up of ordinary citizens from the community where the trial is being held, decides the *verdict* of guilty or innocent. The jurors are chosen at *random* and then questioned by the judge and attorneys to see if they will be able to hear the case fairly. The jury must listen carefully to all the *evidence* and *arguments* presented by the lawyers. Then, after both sides have questioned all the witnesses, the jury goes to a private room to reach a decision. A *foreman*, or speaker, is chosen from the people of the jury. In a criminal case, all the members must agree for a *verdict* to be reached. The jury returns to the courtroom and the *foreman* gives the written decision to the judge.

If the jury decides that the defendant is guilty, the judge sets a date for sentencing. If the jury decides that the defendant is innocent, the defendant is released immediately.

Be a... Journalist!

Kennedy Space Center

Kennedy Space Center is part of **NASA** (National Aeronautics and Space Administration).

Lift off... **We have** *lift off!!!*

President John F. Kennedy made many contributions while he was President. One of them was his expansion of our country's space program. He knew the importance of being a leader in space exploration and he wanted the U.S. to have the best space program in the world.

In 1962, one year after Kennedy was elected president, American astronaut John Glenn piloted the *"Friendship 7"* spacecraft to be the first person to orbit the earth. The spacecraft was launched from Cape Canaveral, Florida, which is located about half-way between Jacksonville and Miami. Cape Canaveral was renamed the John F. Kennedy Space Center in December 1963, to honor the slain president.

Much U.S. history has been made at the Kennedy Space Center. It was the departure site for our first trip to the Moon, and hundreds of scientific and commercial spacecraft. Today, it is the base for Space Shuttle launch and landing operations.

Space exploration continues to be important to America's future. One day, Americans may live among the stars on space stations.

ROCK U.S.A.

Kindness

Acts of kindness *big and small* help make our homes, schools, communities, country and the world a *better place* to live. Do your part, vow to perform five acts of kindness each day. It's not as hard as it sounds. It's as simple as opening a door for someone, paying a compliment, giving words of encouragement or just passing along a *SMILE*.

Be a... Keyboard Player!

Music, like a smile, is the same in all languages!

I wonder if there are other ants out there?

"That's one small step for man one *giant leap* for *mankind*."

Neil Armstrong, 1969
First man to walk on the Moon.

Martin Luther **K**ing, Jr.

Dr. Martin Luther King, Jr. was born in Atlanta, Georgia. He was a leader in the struggle for equal rights for black citizens. He believed in using peaceful ways to change unfair segregation laws.

These laws treated black citizens differently than other citizens. Blacks had to sit in the back of buses in some parts of our country and were not allowed in some public places.

Dr. King gave a famous speech in Washington, D.C., on _August 28, 1963_. It has become known as the _"I Have a Dream"_ speech.

The next year Congress passed a law that prohibited racial discrimination in public places. It also provided for equal opportunities in education and employment.

Dr. King was popular with many people, black and white. But some were angered by his views. He was shot and killed at age 39, in Memphis, Tenn., on April 4, 1968.

The third Monday in January was declared a national holiday in his honor.

Korean War Memorial

Located on the National Mall (near the Lincoln Memorial) in Washington, D.C., is the Korean War Memorial. It is a reminder of the Korean War (1950-53) and the sacrifices and hardships of those who fought and returned, as well as those who fought and lost their lives defending our country. This memorial ensures that those veterans will not be forgotten.

The Memorial consists of a platoon of stainless steel soldiers in the _"Field of Service."_ All four branches of the military are represented by the statues. To the left of the soldiers is a black granite wall. Over two thousand photographs sandblasted into the wall honor the people who provided support to frontline units. Engraved on a nearby wall are the names of the total casualties along with the words...

FREEDOM IS NOT FREE!

Our Space Shuttle fleet includes four orbiters:
Columbia, Discovery, Atlantis and _Endeavour._

The Space Shuttle actually has four major components: two solid rocket boosters, the large orange external tank and the orbiter itself. The entire system weighs about four and a half million pounds at launch. In just eight and a half minutes, the 220,000-pound orbiter goes from a standing start to almost 10 times the speed of a rifle bullet.

President Kennedy was the first president to speak out openly about Civil Rights issues and the contradiction between the status of African Americans and the ideals of freedom.

Literacy Light of Liberty

Literacy

To be productive citizens, effective in the family, the workplace and the community, we must be able to read and write. We must also be able to speak effectively, think creatively, solve problems and use technology to become life-long learners.

The ability to read and write, to understand and be understood, is the foundation of freedom. *Literacy is* the light of liberty and *literacy for all* is the key to America's future.

Abraham Lincoln...

was the 16th president of the United States. He was born in a log cabin in Kentucky in 1809. As a young boy, he loved to read and often borrowed books from his neighbors. Lincoln was President during the Civil War and issued the Emancipation Proclamation that freed the slaves. He was assassinated in 1865 before the war ended. The Lincoln Memorial in Washington, D.C. was built in honor of his memory. His birthday is February 12th and is celebrated on President's Day.

1. 2. 3. 4.

Eleanor Roosevelt, wife of Franklin D. Roosevelt, was the *first* first lady to take stands on controversial issues and become an advocate for human rights. She was the *first* first lady to hold a press conference and the *first* former first lady to be appointed to the United Nations.

THE UNIVERSAL DECLARATION OF **Human Rights**

I READ AND ROCK USA!

I READ AND ROCK USA!

"No one can make you feel inferior without your consent."
Eleanor Roosevelt

"Those who deny freedom to others, deserve it not for themselves; and, under a just God, cannot long retain it."
Abraham Lincoln

Lincoln knew the importance of understanding and being understood. He was a very effective speaker. The *Gettysburg Address* and many of his other speeches and sayings are as meaningful today as they were more than a century ago.

"My American Dream is to become a *Lighthouse Historian*. Lighthouses and their keepers have been important in America's history. They played an important role in the safety of mariners and the growth of the U.S. shipping industry."

L A

Learn from the past - Appreciate th

Reading

helps you soar to new heights and faraway places!

FIRST LADIES

The wife of the President of the United States is called the *First Lady* of our country. Just as a President has goals he wants to accomplish while in office, a *First Lady* has goals that she would like to accomplish too. For example, she might want to improve health care for seniors, protect the rights of children, help the needy or promote literacy for all. Our *First Ladies* have been important in America's history. They have dared to make a difference for our country and its people.

5.   6.   7.   8.

Literacy for all has always been important to *First Lady* Laura Bush, teacher, librarian and wife of 43rd President, George W. Bush.

Which of these *First Ladies*...

- encouraged people to volunteer their services to help others?
- redecorated the White House to make it a center for the arts?
- wanted to help the poor and promoted the *Head Start* program?
- raised awareness about breast cancer to help save lives?
- worked to expand and enforce the rights of children?
- promoted literacy, wrote two books from the family dog's point of view and donated the profits for literacy?
- promoted programs that developed awareness and understanding of mental health issues?
- informed young people about the dangers of drug abuse?

Liberty Bell

The Liberty Bell is a symbol of freedom. It was rung on July 8, 1776 to announce the adoption of the Declaration of Independence. For the next fifty-nine years, it was rung on special occasions and every Fourth of July. Then in 1835, it cracked. No longer rung today, it hangs in the Liberty Bell Pavilion north of Independence Hall in Philadelphia, Pennsylvania. The Liberty Bell Pavilion was opened in 1976, for the nation's bicentennial celebrations. Now, on every Fourth of July, the bell is *rung* (tapped) along with thousands of bells across America.

P★'s ™

Look, Antonio! The Liberty Bell has a *crack*!

It's not *perfect*, Abby, but it's still *special*... just like people.

esent - Preserve the American Dream!

5. Rosalynn Carter promoted mental health awareness. 6. Nancy Reagan educated youth about drug abuse. 7. Barbara Bush promoted literacy. 8. Hillary Clinton wanted more rights for children.

Mount Rushmore

OK, George, so I've never been President, but I *AM* a national symbol!

Mount Rushmore located in the Black Hills of South Dakota is a popular spot for visitors. Each year nearly two million people come to this National Park to see the amazing faces of rock.

Sculptor Gutzon Borglum and nearly 400 workers worked for 14 years to carve the 60-foot-high portraits of four U.S. Presidents:

George Washington
Thomas Jefferson
Theodore Roosevelt and
Abraham Lincoln.

Mount Rushmore was designed to represent the first 150 years of American history. Borglum started drilling into the 6,200-foot mountain in 1927; however, he died in 1941 before it could be completed. Roosevelt's head was not finished when Borglum died. The memorial was finished later that year by his son, Lincoln. Creation of the Shrine of Democracy took 14 years and cost $1 million. Today it is priceless!

Military

With approximately 1.4 million men and women in active duty, and about 654 thousand civilian personnel, the United States Military is the nation's largest employer.

The U.S. military is made up of the Army, Navy, Marine Corps, Air Force and Coast Guard. (The Coast Guard is part of the Department of Transportation during peacetime, but becomes part of the Navy's force in times of war.)

Whether it's saving lives, protecting property, homeland security or keeping the peace, the U.S. military stands ready to keep America **strong and free!**

I'm *proud* to serve my country!

Aye, Aye, Tony!

Money

Money is used to buy things which supports our nation's economy. We have both coins and money made from paper. Money is made by the Bureau of Engraving and Printing. The first U.S. currency made from paper was issued in 1862 to make up for the shortage of coins and to finance the Civil War.

Coins

are made by the U.S. Mint. These coins have the faces of U.S. Presidents on them.

Movie Star!

These are *real* Rock stars!

Mayflower

In 1620, the Pilgrims came from England to America aboard a ship called the Mayflower.

The Pilgrims

left their homes and came to America because they wanted to be free to worship in their own way. On November 11, 1620, before they landed at Plymouth Rock, 41 male Pilgrims signed an agreement. It said that they would set up a government in their new land and obey its laws. This agreement is known as the Mayflower Compact. It later became the foundation of Plymouth's government.

National Parks

Located in Montana, Yellowstone is the first and oldest national park in the world. Here, you can see buffalo and many other wild animals, beautiful scenery and a geyser called Old Faithful.

The National Park Service

manages 384 national parks, monuments, battlefields, historical parks and sites, lakeshores, recreation areas, scenic rivers and trails, and even the White House.

In 1916, Congress passed a law to set up the National Park Service. The mission of the Park Service is to *preserve our natural and historic resources* so everyone can enjoy them now and for years to come.

The ten most visited national parks are:

1. Great Smoky Mountains, NC and TN,
2. Grand Canyon, AZ, 3. Yosemite, CA,
4. Olympic, WA 5. Rocky Mountain, CO
6. Yellowstone, MT, ID, WY
7. Grand Teton, WY 8. Acadia, ME
9. Zion, UT 10. Haleakala, HI

To learn more about the national parklands visit: www.nps.gov

"The Eagle Dance was named for me! *Let's Rock on!*"

ROCK U.S.A

Natural Resources

America is rich in beauty and natural resources. Conservation, protection and management are the keys to making sure that our natural resources will be here for future generations to enjoy. We must all be stewards of our natural resources. Reducing the use of water and electricity and recycling are just a few of the things each of us can do each day to conserve our natural resources.

"Plan to spend some time outdoors *today!*"

WATER   TREES   **CHILDREN** Our Greatest RESOURCE!   ANIMALS   ROCKS AND MINERALS

COPPER   SAND   COA

YELLOWSTONE NATIONAL PARK

Native Americans

For thousands of years the only people to live on the land that is now the United States were Native Americans. America was their land.

Then, beginning in 1492, Europeans arrived in America. Over the centuries, as a result of wars, treaties, policies and diseases brought by the newcomers, the numbers of Native Americans began to decline. Their once large lands were reduced to reservations.

Today, the Native American population of the United States is growing. Native Americans are a diverse group who are part of two worlds, ancient and contemporary. Their culture and heritage play important roles in America's past and present.

Old Faithful

Old Faithful performs 20-23 times a day. People wait patiently with their cameras to see Old Faithful erupt for three to five minutes, spouting water high into the air almost on the hour.

ROCK, you're a GREAT eagle dancer!

Nobel Peace Prize Winner! "Thanks!"

Win the Nobel Peace Prize like former President *Jimmy Carter*.

Learn about the eagle dance at:
http://www.kahokdancers.com/eagle.htm

"Thank you, Mother Nature!"

L/GAS   LAND/SOIL   FISH   PLANTS   WETLANDS

Old Glory

♪♪♪ You're A Grand Old Flag! ♪♪

The term *Old Glory* was first applied to the U.S. flag by a young sea captain who lived in Salem, MA. On his twenty-first birthday, March 17, 1824, Capt. William Driver was presented a beautiful flag by his mother and her sewing group. Driver was delighted with the gift and exclaimed, "I will call her *Old Glory!*" *Old Glory* accompanied the captain on his many voyages.

Before he died he gave the flag to his daughter and said...
"This has been my ship flag, Old Glory. It has been my constant companion. I love it as a mother loves her child. Cherish it, as I have cherished it."

The flag remained in the Driver family until 1922. It was then sent to the Smithsonian Museum in Washington, D.C.

Today, our country's flag is often referred to as Old Glory.
Long may she wave!

OLYMPIC GAMES

Many young Americans have dreams of being Olympic athletes.

The Olympic Games provide an opportunity for young athletes around the world to meet and compete in a variety of sports in the spirit of peace.

USA 〇〇〇〇〇

There are two types of Olympic Games, the Summer Olympic Games and the Winter Olympic Games. They are held on alternate even-numbered years at different sites. For example, the Summer Olympic Games were held in 2000 and the Winter Olympic Games were held in 2002. The Olympic Games are administered by the International Olympic Committee which is headquartered in Lausanne, Switzerland.

The modern Olympic Games began in Athens, Greece, in 1896, two years after French educator Pierre de Coubertin proposed that the Olympic Games of ancient Greece be revived to promote a more peaceful world.

The Olympic Games continue to promote <u>peace</u> and <u>world</u> <u>understanding</u>!

Products made in the USA!

Own Your Own Business! STORE

Old Ironsides

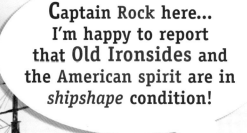

> Captain Rock here...
> I'm happy to report
> that Old Ironsides and
> the American spirit are in
> *shipshape* condition!

U.S.S. Constitution

The ***U.S.S. Constitution*** is a wooden hull, three-masted frigate (a high-speed medium-sized sailing vessel) and is called *"Old Ironsides"* because bullets could not go through her tough oak sides. She was one of *six* original frigates that formed the U.S. Navy and was used to fight against the Barbary pirates.

"Old Ironsides" has 44-guns and was built in Boston, MA, in 1797. The ship was scheduled to be scrapped in 1830, but Oliver Wendell Holmes' poem *"Old Ironsides"* inspired a public movement to save it. Restored in 1925, the *U.S.S. Constitution* is now the oldest commissioned vessel in the U.S. Navy. She is presently moored at the Charleston Navy Yard in Boston and serves as a museum ship.

Oath

I promise to preserve, protect and defend...

To take an Oath *is to make a promise.*

<u>*When someone becomes President*</u> they must make a promise called the oath of office. The new President promises to preserve, protect and defend the Constitution of the United States.

<u>*A person testifying in court*</u> must also take an oath and promise to *tell the truth, the whole truth and nothing but the truth.*

<u>*The Olympic Oath*</u> is taken in the name of all the athletes by a member of the host's team. The athletes state their commitment to the ideals of <u>*sportsmanship*</u> in competition.

First Woman Presid*Ant?*

The crew of Old Ironsides included 450 men and boys. She traveled at 13+ knots (approximately 15 miles per hour).

Patriotism
Key To Freedom

Patriotism is...

showing love, loyalty and devotion for our country and to the values and principles of democracy upon which it depends.

There are many ways that citizens can show patriotism. We show patriotism when we display the flag, say the *Pledge of Allegiance*, vote or join the military to defend our country and our *freedom*.

We can also show patriotism by supporting the leaders of our country and volunteering our time to support our community, charities and other worthy causes.

President

To become President of the United States, a person must be born a U.S. citizen. He or she must be at least 35 years old and must have lived in the United States for at least 14 years.

The President is elected by the vote of American citizens and serves four years. Then he or she has to run again to be elected for another four years. A President can only serve eight years or two terms.

The Seal of the President of the United States

was adopted by Executive Order of President Harry S. Truman on October 25, 1945. The Presidential Seal is used on official envelopes containing messages or other documents from the President. It is also found on many things the President uses, such as his desk, car, "Air Force One" and speaking podium.

Peace

Anyone born a U.S. citizen can **become President** of the United States of America!

"My *AMERICAN* Dream is to be...

AbrahANT Lincoln

FOUR SCORE AND SEVEN YEARS AGO...

PRESIDENT OF THE UNITED STATES."

Pilgrims

MAYFLOWER 1620

"No TyrANTS Here, Abby!"

PLYMOUTH ROCK

The Pilgrims came to America on the *Mayflower* in 1620. They were willing to leave their homes in England and make the long, dangerous journey across the Atlantic Ocean to have religious freedom. Today, many people from other countries immigrate to America to share our freedoms.

Patriot

Patrick Henry   Nathan Ha

These men were three of the many brave *patriots* whose beliefs helped form our nation. They were brave an willing to *stand up* for these beliefs, fight and even give their lives for *freedom* and *democracy!*

POLITICAL PARTIES

A political party is a group of people who try to win elections to run the government. We have two major political parties in the United States. Most Americans support either the Republican or the Democratic Party. Some people are Independents. They feel so strongly about an issue or candidate that they join a party other than the two *"biggies."* The elephant is the symbol of the Republican Party and the donkey is the symbol of the Democratic Party. These symbols were made popular during the 1870s by political cartoonist Thomas Nast. Mr. Nast, a Republican, used the donkey to make fun of the Democrats and before long, the Democratic Party was stuck with that symbol. People form new political parties when they have ideas and beliefs that are different from the parties in power. We have had lots of political parties over the years, the Whigs, the Bull Moose and the Know-Nothing Party to name a few.

"Let's ROLL!"

George W. Bush, **43rd President** of the United States... is the son of former President, George Bush.

The only other father and son to serve as U.S. Presidents were John Adams and John Quincy Adams.

Be TRUE to the *red, white* and *blue!*

Which of the Presidents on this page:
- loved jelly beans and was the oldest man to be elected President?
- was our only President to be adopted?
- was a peanut farmer?
- was the youngest torpedo bomber pilot in the navy during World War II?
- was the only President to be a Rhodes Scholar?

Pioneers

A *pioneer* is someone who ventures into unknown or unclaimed territory.

Pioneers settled the American West.

They packed all they could into wagons, left their homes and loved ones behind, crossed mountains, rivers and plains to make new homes and seek their fortunes. Today, proof of their determination and hard work is seen everywhere in U.S. cities and towns they helped build.

ul Revere

PATRIOTS... re colonists who ted freedom from land for the colonies.

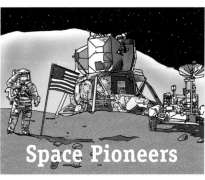

THE FUTURE

Space Pioneers

John Glenn, was the *first American* to orbit the earth.
Neil Armstrong was the *first American* to walk on the moon.

Great American

Quotes

Quotes inspire us, help us to better understand life, ourselves and others...

"The terrorists attacked us for what we have done *right* - not for what we may have done wrong. Indeed, we have created a society in which there is more liberty and more prosperity than any country on Earth - past or present."

Norman Podhoretz
Author

"Ask NOT what your country can do for you... but what you can do for your country!"
John F. Kennedy

"We have been blessed with the opportunity to stand for something... for liberty, freedom and fairness."
Ronald Reagan

"Everyone has the power for greatness, not fame, but for greatness, because greatness is determined by service."
Dr. Martin Luther King, Jr.

True patriotism celebrates America - a nation that is united as one people, the descendants of many cultures, races, religions and ethnic groups.

The United States is a unique nation. It is not based on ethnic kinship but on a set of ideas. It is not about how we are alike or different, but what we can do to make a difference in our own life and in the lives of those around us.

"Your personal daily effort is your living legacy - to your family and to your community... It is your individual signature on the *History of America*."

John Mooy
Author and Storyteller

"It is not fair to ask of others what you are not willing to do yourself."
Eleanor Roosevelt

"America lives in the heart of every man everywhere who wishes to find a place where he will be free to work out his destiny as he chooses."
Woodrow Wilson

"They have achieved success who have gained the love of children; who have left the world better than they found it; who have looked for the best in others and have given the best they had."
A. J. Stanley

Quality
Made in USA

Buying American made products is good for all Americans!

Clothes...   Cars...   Furniture...   Homes...   Medical Care...   Electronics...   Services.

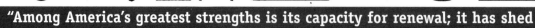

"Never doubt that a small group of committed citizens can change the world. Indeed, it is the only thing that ever has." - Margaret Mead

Quilt

Quilting has always been a part of America's history and culture. Quilting is an art form and a means of expressing one's creativity. Through the years, quilting was also a way of using cloth scraps and parts of worn-out clothing to make warm and pretty bedcovers. Quilting parties also provided a time for women to get together to share a common interest and to socialize.

During the days of the Underground Railroad, due to the need for secrecy, escape information was passed along to the slaves seeking freedom by using quilts. Different quilt patterns are said to have had certain meanings, messages and directions. The star pattern symbolized the north star that the slaves followed north... to freedom.

"The pen... than... *is* mightier the sword."

Quill

"**Freedom** is the last **best hope.**"
Abraham Lincoln

A quill pen was made from a feather and then dipped into ink. Both making the quill pen and writing with it were arts.

Like many other famous documents the Declaration of Independence and the Constitution were both written and signed with a quill pen. The word *"pen"* comes from the Latin word *"penna"* which means *"feather."*

"Educate the children of a democracy and the democracy will prosper."
- E.C.S.

FAMOUS QUOTES

"The *American Dream* endures."
Jimmy Carter

"*Sew well* and you shall *reap well*!"

Be a Great Quilter!

The American People!

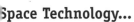
Space Technology...

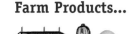
Farm Products...

Education...
SCHOOL

"To succeed, jump as quickly at opportunities as you do to conclusions." – *Benjamin Franklin*

Revolutionary

"Listen my children and you shall hear, of the midnight ride of Paul Revere..." from Paul Revere's Ride, a poem by Henry Wadsworth Longfellow.

In December 1776,

the American Revolution was not going well for the Americans. The soldiers were discouraged and General George Washington desperately needed a victory. Christmas was coming and Washington knew that the 1,200 German soldiers (Hessians), who were fighting for the British, would be busy celebrating Christmas, so he planned a surprise attack and was determined to defeat them.

On Christmas evening, Washington and 2,700 men, some who were shoeless in the freezing weather, crossed the icy Delaware River and surprised the Hessians and won the battle. The Battle of Trenton was a major turning point in the American Revolution.

King George III became King of England in 1760, at age 22, after his grandfather King George II died. He was very disliked by the American colonists.

In 1763, England wanted the colonists to help pay for the French and Indian War. King George III *levied* a series of taxes on the American colonists. Taxes were put on things the colonists needed, like tea and sugar.

The colonists began to protest about the taxes. They did not think they should be taxed because they were not represented in the British Parliament.

Soon, what began as a protest against taxation without representation ended in a war for freedom and independence. George Washington was chosen to lead the Continental Army.

The Revolutionary War began with the Battles of Lexington and Concord on April 19, 1775, and ended with the signing of the Treaty of Paris in 1783.

America became a *free nation!*

Paul Revere

Paul Revere is a famous American patriot. He was a silversmith in Boston by trade. He belonged to the secret patriot organization the Sons of Liberty, and was an excellent horseman.

On the evening of April 18,1775, Paul Revere, with the help of William Dawes, made a famous ride to Lexington to warn Samuel Adams and John Hancock that British troops were coming to arrest them. On the way, Revere stopped at each house to give the news. A few days later, the battle on Lexington Green marked the beginning of the Revolutionary War.

"The Midnight Ride of *Paul Revere!*"

Be a... Rancher! "Yeeha!"

We *herd* it was a great occupation!

General George Washington crossing the icy Delaware River in the winter of 1776.

By *George*, I think you've *got it...* A *BIG surprise* for the *Redcoats!*

Many of the American troops who fought in the Battle of Trenton had no shoes and were barefoot in the freezing weather or wrapped rags around their feet.

Representative Government

Representative government was established in the Constitution. It is one in which citizens elect others to act for them in government. Elected officials represent citizens' interests, make and enforce laws for them as individuals and for the common good. We choose the people we want to represent us in government by *voting*.

It is important for all citizens to vote in every election. Persons who do not vote lose their voice in government.

WE THE PEOPLE

REPRESENTATIVE

STATE AND FEDERAL GOVERNMENT

Recycle

We conserve <u>natural resources</u> such as timber, water and minerals when we *recycle.*
Recycling helps reduce pollution of our air and water, saves energy and reduces the amount of greenhouse gases and has many other positive effects on our environment.
Recycling is important to the future of America. Do your part to help. *Remember the power of one!*

RESELL OLD FURNITURE   HAVE A SCHOOL PAPER DRIVE!   GARAGE SALE!   PLASTIC BOTTLES   RECYCLED METAL   RECYCLED GLASS   CLOTHES   Toys   CANS   OLD TIRES   CAR BATTERIES

NO TOXIC WASTE

STATUE OF LIBERTY

The Statue Of Liberty is a symbol of freedom throughout the world. It stands on Liberty Island in New York Harbor. This 305-foot copper statue is one of the world's largest. It is as tall as a 15-story building and weighs as much as 37 elephants.

The Statue of Liberty was given to the United States by France on July 4, 1884 as a gift of friendship. It was given in memory of the *alliance* (friendship) between France and the American colonists during the Revolutionary War. It was opened to visitors in 1886.

Lady Liberty has a crown with seven rays. The rays stand for the seven seas and seven continents. Her torch is a symbol that welcomes immigrants and visitors to our country. The broken chain at her feet is a symbol of freedom. She holds a tablet in her hand with the date of the Declaration of Independence. Liberty's mouth is three feet wide, each eye is two feet, six inches across and her forefinger is eight feet long! School children in France saved pennies to help pay for the statue. In 1986, to celebrate the 100th anniversary of the Statue of Liberty, school children across America donated pennies to help pay for repairs to the statue during her restoration.

OH- - say! can you see,

Star-Spangled Banner

The *Star-Spangled Banner* was written by Francis Scott Key in 1814, after he watched the night-time battle between England and America from a ship in Baltimore harbor. He was very excited when the American flag was still flying over Fort McHenry in the morning.

A special poem is <u>written on the base</u> of the Statue of Liberty:

"Give me your tired, your poor,
Your huddled masses yearning to breathe free,
The wretched refuse of your teeming shore.
Send these, the homeless, tempest-tost to me,
I lift my lamp beside the golden door!"

Emma Lazarus

Who said, "A penny saved is a penny earned?"

I think it was Benjamin Frank*lANT*, Abby!

Be a... MARS

SPACE EXPLORER

Senators

Each state has two U.S. Senators that are elected by the people to serve in Congress. A Senator must be 30 years old and must have been a U.S. citizen for nine years. Senators serve six-year terms. They do not all run for re-election at the same time. One-third of the members run every two years. Senators from the same state do not run at the same time.

The first woman to be elected to the U.S. Senate was Hattie Wyatt Caraway of Arkansas in 1932.

Stat

Congress adopted the *Star-Spangled Banner* as our National Anthem in **1931.**

by the dawn's ear- ly light,

Immigrants
coming to America competed to be the first to spot the *Statue of Liberty.*

Supreme Court of the United States

Located in Washington D.C., near the Capitol, the Supreme Court Building has housed the Supreme Court since 1935. The Supreme Court is the highest court in our country. It is part of the Judicial Branch of our government. There are nine judges (Justices) on the Court. One of these is the Chief Justice. The Justices are chosen by the President and confirmed (voted on) by the members of the Senate.

"Judges, therefore, should always be men of learning and experience in the laws, of exemplary minds, great patience, calmness, coolness and attention..."
John Adams, 1776

ROCK ON
Lady LIBERTY!

Let's go on a nature walk in the park!

Liberty

ROCK U.S.A

SAFE

"Safe World
for Children and All Living Things!"
Americans want their children to live and grow up in a safe and happy environment where they can enjoy all the blessings of freedom. This is our hope for ALL children...
EVERYWHERE!

Transportat

The increased ability to communicate, travel and ship products has increased the growth and prosperity of our country.

Americans first traveled on foot at the pace they could walk. Later they traveled along muddy, rocky trails beside their wagons or carts. Others, who lived near water, moved at the speed they could float or paddle canoes.

Water was our country's first system of roads. Boats transported both people and products. Then came stagecoaches and trains. After the building of the Transcontinental Railroad, which connected the eastern and western U.S., people could travel most everywhere by train.

Then came automobiles, trucks, motorcycles and other motorized vehicles that provide a way to travel and ship goods across the country.

Today airplanes and ships allow Americans to travel and transport merchandise around the world.

Transportation and communication are important to our country's economy.

Large freighters up to *1,000 feet long* transport products on the *Great Lakes.*

Cars were a *revolution* in transportation. They gave Americans the freedom to travel whenever they wanted! Cars brought about drive-in movie theaters, drive-in restaurants and roadside motels. Cars continue to be important in the everyday life of most Americans and to our nation's economy.

First Oldsmobile 1897

Trains

In 1862, Abraham Lincoln signed the Pacific Railway Act to build the *Transcontinental Railroad.* The Central Pacific Railroad and the Union Pacific Railroad met at Promontory Point, Utah on May 10, 1869. A golden spike joined the two railways. Americans could now travel from coast to coast by tra It was a great day in our history.

Trucks

Trucks transport many *American* products across the country every day!

Trail of Tears

In 1838, the United States government removed more than 16,000 Cherokee Indian people from their homelands in Tennessee, Alabama, North Carolina and Georgia and sent them to Indian Territory (today known as Oklahoma). Hundreds died during the trip west, and thousands more perished due to relocation. Today the *Trail of Tears* is a National Historic Trail. It covers about 2,200 miles of land and water routes, and crosses parts of nine states. It helps us remember those who died during this sad time in America's history.

Teachers

Teachers have the most important job in our country... educating *America's children!*

"These were the original BIG wheels!"

Bicycles

In
December, 1903,
Orville and Wilbur Wright
were the first to fly a controlled aircraft.

This is a...
golden day
in
transportation history!

T ractors greatly improved *American farming!*

"We all have a BIG stake in *FREEDOM!*"

1869. May 10th. 1869.
GREAT EVENT
Rail Road from the Atlantic to the Pacific
GRAND OPENING
OF THE
Union Pacific
RAIL ROAD,
PLATTE VALLEY ROUTE.
PASSENGER TRAINS LEAVE
OMAHA
ON THE ARRIVAL OF TRAINS FROM THE EAST
THROUGH TO SAN FRANCISCO
In less than Four Days, avoiding the Dangers of the Sea!
Travelers for Pleasure, Health or Business
LUXURIOUS CARS & EATING HOUSES
ON THE UNION PACIFIC RAIL ROAD.
PULLMAN'S PALACE SLEEPING CARS
RUN WITH ALL THROUGH PASSENGER TRAINS.
GOLD, SILVER AND OTHER MINERS!
CHEYENNE for DENVER, CENTRAL CITY & SANTA FE
THROUGH TICKETS FOR SALE AT ALL PRINCIPAL RAILROAD OFFICES
Be Sure they Read via Platte Valley or Omaha

Harley-Davidson®
Walter Davidson Sr., William A. Davidson, Arthur Davidson and William S. Harley, Milwaukee mechanics and inventors, came upon the idea to motorize a bike and the *Harley-Davidson Motor Company* was born. Nicknamed "American Iron," Harley-Davidson® motorcycles are steeped in American tradition and tell the story of a company that "endured to succeed" and one that serves as a model of *American pride* and the *American dream.*

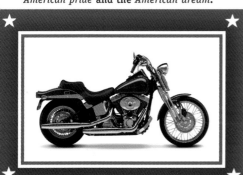

Telegraph

The first electric telegraph was constructed between Washington and Baltimore in 1844. Soon the entire U.S. had an instant means of communication. Now, the only thing separating the U.S. from Europe was 2,000 miles of Atlantic Ocean. On July 13, 1866, after many tries, the transatlantic cable was successfully laid by the *Great Eastern*, a magnificent ship of its day.

"Pay it out, Oh! Pay it out. As long as you are able; For if you put the darned brakes on... POP goes the cable."

The Great Eastern

U.S. Postal

The **U.S. Postal Service** issues special stamps to commemorate American people and events.

"Those stamps really look familiar!"

In the early colonial times, people depended on friends, merchants and Native Americans to carry messages between the colonies.

On July 6, 1775, members of the Second Continental Congress agreed that a Postmaster General be appointed for the United States. Benjamin Franklin was appointed to the position. This was the birth of the Post Office Department, now the U.S. Postal Service. It is the second oldest department or agency of the U.S. Franklin is credited with establishing a system more than two centuries ago that has performed very well for the American people.

Today, the Postal Service delivers hundreds of millions of messages and billions of dollars in financial transactions each day to eight million businesses and...
280 million Americans.

U.S.MAIL

Underground Railroad

The *Underground Railroad* was neither underground nor a railroad, but a secret network of safe houses and antislavery activists... black, white and Native American, who helped slaves escape to freedom. Every home that welcomed runaways and every individual who offered food, clothing or other assistance could be considered part of the railroad. Though never formally organized, tens of thousands of slaves, aided by more than 3,200 railroad "workers," escaped to the northern states, Canada, Texas, Mexico and through Florida to the Caribbean.

Service

First AIRMAIL STAMP

The *eagle*...
has landed!
I have an airmail letter
for a...
Mr. Franklin.

The Pony Express

The *Pony Express Trail* was used by young men on fast paced horses to carry the nation's mail across the country, from St. Joseph, Missouri to Sacramento, California, in only 10 days. Organized by private entrepreneurs, the horse-and-rider relay system became the nation's most direct and practical means of east-west communications before the telegraph. It was only in operation for 18 months, but proved that a central overland transportation route was possible.

The first U.S. airmail pilot.

Uncle Sam

I WANT YOU for the U.S. ARMY ENLIST NOW

The white-haired, bearded character known as Uncle Sam is a symbol of the United States. He wears an eye-catching suit of red and white striped pants, a blue jacket and a top hat with a band of stars. His name came from the letters *U* and *S*, a short way to say the United States. The character became popular when he was used on posters during World War I to recruit young men to join the army.

United Nations

In 1945, immediately after World War II, an international organization with the goal to keep global peace was born.
It was called the *United Nations* and replaced the former *League of Nations*.
In the beginning, members consisted of 51 nations.
Today over 188 nations join forces in keeping the world at peace.

USA Freedom Corps

This organization was formed when President George W. Bush called upon every American to get involved in strengthening America's communities and sharing America's compassion around the world by volunteering service to others. Whether it be mentoring a child, caring for an elderly neighbor, teaching someone to read, or donating food and clothing to those in need, the USA Freedom Corps is about helping others.

FREEDOM

"Neither snow, nor rain, nor heat, nor gloom of night stays these couriers from the swift completion of their appointed rounds."

Veterans

One year after World War I drew to a close, President Woodrow Wilson declared November 11, 1919, as **Armistice Day...** a national holiday to celebrate victory "in the war to end all wars". Yet the dream of world peace was soon lost as first World War II and then the Korean Conflict called America's troops back to war.

Congress voted Armistice Day a national holiday in 1938. It was renamed as...

Veterans Day in 1954, as a tribute to all the men and women who have defended the cause of freedom around the world.

On November 11 each year Americans still give thanks for peace. There are ceremonies and speeches and at 11:00 AM, most Americans observe a moment of silence, remembering those who fought for peace and freedom.

Victory Gardens

It was World War II and United States citizens were asked to do their part at home to help fund the war. Over 20 million home-owners plowed up their lawns to plant vegetables, fruits and berries, with amazing results. In 1943 alone, Victory Gardens produced more than 40 percent of all produce consumed in our country. This freed up tons of food supplies to feed the troops at home and abroad.

Today many people in large American cities plant vegetable gardens in vacant city lots to

help feed those in need.

Hey, TONY! Our garden is a victory!

Yes, Abby! We are pl*ant*-n ants!

Vietnam Women's Memorial

Nearly 10,000 women in uniform actually served in Vietnam during the conflict. They completed their tours of duty and made a difference. Many gave their lives.

The Vietnam Women's Memorial was established not only to honor those women who served, but also for the families who lost loved ones in the war, so they would know about the women who provided comfort, care, and a human touch for those who were suffering and dying.

The Vietnam Women's Memorial was dedicated in 1993 as part of the Vietnam Veterans Memorial.

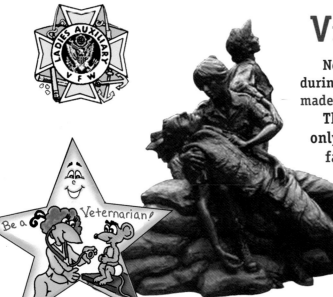

Be a Veternarian!

Vietnam Veterans Memorial

So many names, so many brave American men and women.

(58,178 American men and women lost their lives during the war in Vietnam.)

The Vietnam Veterans Memorial located near the Lincoln Memorial in Washington D.C. honors the U.S. men and women who served their country and lost their lives during the Vietnam War. Its polished, black granite walls are inscribed with the names of the dead, listed *chronologically* by date of casualty. A list of those missing in action is also inscribed. A life-size statue of three servicemen stands near the V-shaped walls.

Vice Presidents

According to the U.S. Constitution, the *Vice President* of the United States serves as the President of the Senate. The Vice President also assumes the duties of the President if the President is unable to serve.

Vice President Andrew Johnson, was the *first Vice President* to assume the presidency. He became President when President Abraham Lincoln was assassinated in 1865.

Vote!

We choose people to represent us in local, state and national government by exercising our right to vote. Voting is a right provided to American citizens by the United States Constitution. All American citizens 18 years or older can vote. Voting is one of the most important things Americans can do to keep our country *strong.*

Washington, D.C.

Washington, D.C.,

was established as our nation's capital in 1800 and is named for George Washington. He actually chose the site along the Potomac River where the new city was to be built.

The city was built to be the seat of the United States government and government business happens everyday in many buildings in Washington, D.C.

The White House, Capitol building, Supreme Court, Pentagon, Library of Congress, National Archives Building and the Bureau of Engraving are just a few of the places where the work of our government takes place.

Washington, D.C. also has many beautiful parks, monuments, memorials and museums. These are visited by millions of people each year.

The Smithsonian museums (all 14 of them) hold many of our nation's treasures. The most popular is the National Air and Space Museum which attracts 10 million visitors each year.

People also come to see the pandas at Washington's National Zoo. Others like to visit the Kennedy Center for the Performing Arts, the Washington Cathedral and Ford's Theatre.

Our nation's capital is a city of... historical <u>sites</u> and beautiful <u>sights</u>!

Welcome to *Eagle-Eye Tours*. I'm Rock USA, your tour guide. Today we will be visiting our *nation's capital.*

We the People

Suffragettes wanted the right to vote!

Official Program WOMAN SUFFRAGE Procession

Washington D.C. March 3, 1913

Mr. PRESIDENT HOW LONG MUST WOMEN WAIT FOR LIBERTY

Mr. PRESIDENT WHAT WILL YOU DO FOR WOMAN SUFFRAGE

Women's Suffrage

Before 1920, women could not vote in our country.
Many women worked for many years to change this.

Susan B. Anthony, Lucretia Mott, Martha Wright, Elizabeth Cady Stanton, Mary Ann McClintock and Sojourner Truth are only a few of the brave women who worked tirelessly to get the U.S. Congress to add an amendment to the Constitution that would allow women to vote.

In August, 1920 the nineteenth Amendment was added to the Constitution granting women the right to vote.

Our Nation's Capital

The White House

The *President* and the *first family* live in the White House during the presidency. George Washington chose the site, but the first President to live in the White House was John Adams. Construction began in 1792 and was completed in 1800.
The President's Oval Office is in the White House.
The White House is also referred to as the Executive Mansion. It has 107 rooms and is located at 1600 Pennsylvania Avenue NW.

Washington Monument

The Washington Monument is an *obelisk*. An *obelisk* has four sides that slope up to a point.

"Great... Bioindex!"

Washington Monument

The Washington Monument was built in memory of George Washington, the first president of the United States. Construction began in 1848, but was not completed until 1884. At 555 feet tall, it is one of the tallest *masonry* (stone, brick or concrete) structures on earth. It is Washington's only skyscraper and can be seen from many miles.

The British attacked Washington in 1814 and burned the Executive Mansion. When it was rebuilt, the house was painted *white* to cover the scorched stone.

X · out

Though we live in the greatest country in the world, we still have work to do to make our country even better. Today, many children in America go to bed hungry. Many adults cannot read or write. Some people do not like others because they are different. Some people lack pride in their jobs. Many people cannot afford proper health care and drugs and crime are problems in many of our great cities.

Private citizens and government officials must work together to improve these issues. Each of us can help by gaining a better understanding of these problems. Education is the key. *Remember the power of one...* "I am but one, I cannot do everything, but I can do something..." Vow to do *something* <u>today</u> to help Rock U.S.A.™!

The talking is over let's do it... for *America*!

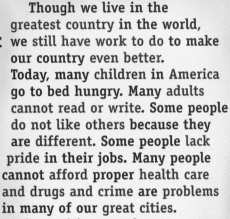

X = unknown

$$X \times X = X^2$$
$$X + Y = Z$$

X is used as an unknown in some mathematical equations.

Roman Numeral
X=10 X stands for...

the number ten when written as a Roman numeral. This numbering system was made by the ancient Romans. Roman numerals are used in the Constitution for articles and amendment numbers (such as Article X and Amendment IX) and as dates on buildings. There are seven characters used in Roman numerals:

I = 1   V = 5   X = 10   L = 50
C = 100   D = 500   M = 1000

DR~~U~~GS HUN~~G~~ER APA~~T~~HY

BUL~~L~~YING CR~~I~~ME DISE~~A~~SE

Discrim~~i~~ination DISRE~~S~~PECT

HA~~T~~E Hypo~~c~~risy Illite~~r~~acy

Medi~~o~~crity PREJ~~U~~DICE

TERR~~O~~RISM TYRA~~N~~NY

VIOL~~E~~NCE

POV~~E~~RTY ABU~~U~~SE

Treasure Map

X - Marks the spot!

It is said that many, many years ago when there were pirates sailing the seas, they would often take their treasure and bury it. To remember where to find it when they returned, they drew a map and marked the hiding place with an X. Today, we still mark some things with an X to indicate their importance.

The letters X and O can mean hugs and kisses! ⊗ ⊗ ⊗

Xmas Holidays

Early Christians used an X as a symbol for Christ. Today an X is often used in the abbreviation for the word *Christmas*. Not all Americans celebrate Christmas, but many Americans do celebrate Christmas on December 25th.

e things that count can't be counted." - Albert Einstein

In the early days of our country many people could not read or write. They used an "X" to sign their names on legal documents and to vote.

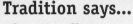

Yankee Do

"Well, *shucks*,
we should thank that
Redcoat, Dr. Schuckburg,
for giving us a *GREAT*
marching song!"

Visit... Yellowstone National Park!

A great
*American
Dream...*
visit our
National
Parks!

Tradition says...

that *Yankee Doodle* may
have been written during the
French and Indian War. When
the colonists, dressed in buckskin
and fur, joined Braddock's English
forces at Niagara they looked a lot
different than the English who
wore fancy uniforms into battle.

Dr. Richard Schuckburg, a
British army surgeon, is said to
have written the tune in the 1750s
to "make fun" of the colonial
"country bumpkins."
By the time of the American
Revolution, however, the colonials
had changed the words to the
catchy tune and taken it as their
own... **marching song.**

The word macaroni
mentioned in the song Yankee Doodle,
refers to a fancy, overdressed ("dandy")
style of Italian clothing
worn by many English gentlemen
at the time.

The
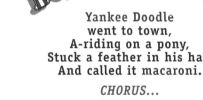
Yankee Doodle Song!

Yankee Doodle
went to town,
A-riding on a pony,
Stuck a feather in his hat,
And called it macaroni.

CHORUS...

*Yankee Doodle, keep it up,
Yankee Doodle dandy,
Mind the music and the step,
And with the girls be handy.*

Father and I went down to camp
Along with Captain Gooding
And there we saw the men and boys
As thick as hasty pudding.

REPEAT CHORUS

There was Captain Washington
Upon a slapping stallion
A-giving orders to his men
I guess there was a million.

REPEAT CHORUS

Dr. Richard Schuckburg

And called
it...
spaghetti!

"Doesn't he look *dandy*?"

No, Tony!
It's...
macaroni!

**Young Women's
Christian Association**

Helping to build...
**strong kids,
strong families,
strong communities!**

The **Y**

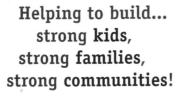

The **YMCA** - (Young Men's Christian Association)
was founded in London England in 1844
by *Sir George Williams.*

The organization was formed because of unhealthy
social conditions at the end of England's Industrial
Revolution. The YMCA came to America before the Civil War.
Its mission is to put christian principles into practice
through programs that build healthy spirit, mind and body.

YWCA - Providing women and girls with the
information they need to deal with critical issues in their lives:
childcare and youth development, housing and shelter, economic
empowerment, leadership development, global awareness, health
and fitness, racial justice and human rights, and violence prevention.

YUKON GOLD RUSH

In 1897 there was a gold strike in the Yukon
Territory. From 1897 to 1898, tens of thousands
of people from across the United States and
around the world stopped in Seattle on the way
to the Yukon to "strike it rich." Here the hopeful
miners purchased millions of dollars in food,
clothing, equipment, pack animals and steamship
tickets. This *great stampede of people* helped
shape the Seattle we know today. This *same
stampede of people* also traveled through Alaska
on their way to the gold fields. This caused
Congress to have to establish laws in the Territory.

YUKON TERRITORY

Zones AND Zip

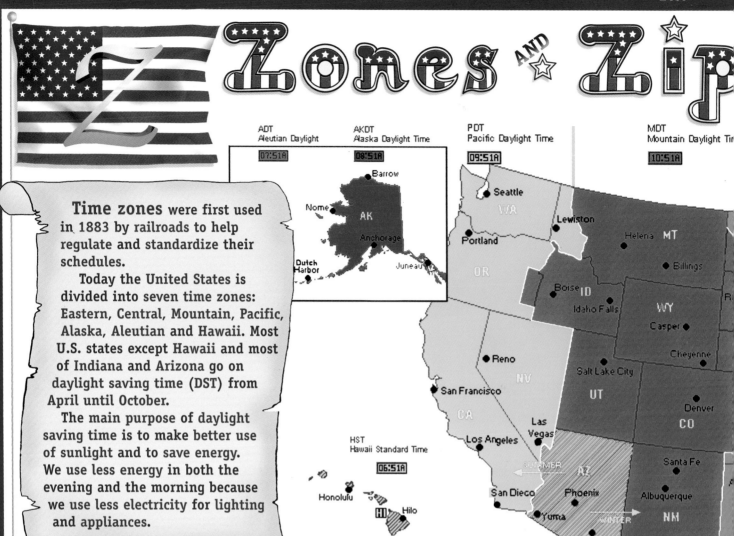

Time zones were first used in 1883 by railroads to help regulate and standardize their schedules.

Today the United States is divided into seven time zones: Eastern, Central, Mountain, Pacific, Alaska, Aleutian and Hawaii. Most U.S. states except Hawaii and most of Indiana and Arizona go on daylight saving time (DST) from April until October.

The main purpose of daylight saving time is to make better use of sunlight and to save energy. We use less energy in both the evening and the morning because we use less electricity for lighting and appliances.

ADT Aleutian Daylight · AKDT Alaska Daylight Time · PDT Pacific Daylight Time · MDT Mountain Daylight Time

07:51A · 08:51A · 09:51A · 10:51A

HST Hawaii Standard Time · 06:51A

SUMMER ← · WINTER →

Temperature Zones

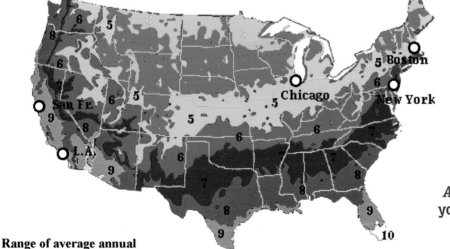

The temperature and weather across the United States are about as diverse as the people. Temperature and weather determine where we live, what we wear, what we grow and many other things that affect our daily lives.

I have the *ANT*swers to your weather questions.

Range of average annual minimum temperatures

Zone	(F)	(C)
Zone 3	(-35 F)	(-37 C)
Zone 4	(-25 F)	(-32 C)
Zone 5	(-15 F)	(-26 C)
Zone 6	(-5 F)	(-21 C)
Zone 7	(5 F)	(-15 C)
Zone 8	(15 F)	(-9 C)
Zone 9	(25 F)	(-4 C)
Zone 10	(35 F)	(+2 C)

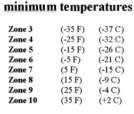

Be a... Zoo Keeper! "Grrrr!"

Codes

The first digit in the Zip Code indicates the geographical area of the United States (Beginning at zero for the Northeast and going to nine for the far West). For example, ZIP codes in Augusta, Maine start with 04330 and those in Los Angeles, California start with 90001.

USE ZIP CODE.

CDT Central Daylight Time
`11:51A`

EDT Eastern Daylight
`12:51P`

If the New York Yankees are playing at home and the game is televised live, beginning at 6:00pm, Eastern time, Yankee fans in San Francisco would watch the game at 3:00pm Pacific time.

By July, 1963, five-digit **ZIP codes...** (Zoning Improvement Plan codes) had been assigned to every address throughout the United States. The large increase in the amount of mail, transportation needs and the cost to sort and deliver our nation's mail had made it necessary to switch to modern technology to make this process easier and more efficient.

This *unique timepiece* works well in *ANY* time zone!

Washington National Zoo

Many people come to the Washington National Zoo each year. Most of them come to see the pandas. Pandas are *endangered*. There are only about 1,000 left in the wild and about 140 in zoos. Panda experts at the National Zoo, San Diego Zoo and Atlanta Zoo study pandas in the hope that they can learn how to increase their numbers to avoid *extinction*.

giraffes and many other animals and plants. There is also an Amazon exhibit with a tropical forest and river.

Core Democratic Values

CORE DEMOCRATIC VALUES are the fundamental beliefs and constitutional principles of American society which unite all Americans. These values are expressed in the Declaration of Independence, the United States Constitution and other significant documents, speeches and writings of the nation.

LIFE

We have the right to live and be safe. Rules keep us safe, and we must follow them. LIFE, protected by the Federal Constitution, includes all personal rights and their enjoyment; rights to marry, establish a home, bring up children, freedom of worship, occupation, speech, assembly and press.

LIBERTY

LIBERTY is the freedom to think, act and be yourself. Follow your beliefs and let others follow theirs. Liberty is freedom from governmental interference in personal, political and economic activities.

PURSUIT OF HAPPINESS

You may do what makes you happy as long as it does not hurt others. Have fun, but follow the rules at home and school. American citizens have the right to seek happiness if they do not infringe upon others' rights.

COMMON GOOD

COMMON GOOD is good for all. People have a responsibility to others. People often give up some personal freedoms for the good of a larger group of people. Whenever we do something kind or helpful to others we are contributing to the common good.

JUSTICE

JUSTICE is being fair.
All United States citizens are to be treated fairly.

DIVERSITY

Everyone is different. Work and play with everyone. America is a mixture of different cultures blended together with equal liberties under the law. Our different backgrounds helped build our country and make it strong.

EQUALITY

Everyone is equal. Give everyone an equal chance. All United States citizens are to be treated the same under the law.

TRUTH

" I do! "

Tell the truth.
American democracy depends on people telling the truth in court, in government, in the news and to each other.

POPULAR SOVEREIGNTY

The majority RULES!

PEOPLE'S VOTE

Americans vote.
Majority rules.
American Government is ruled by the people through their *vote*.

I'm Patriotic to the core!

PATRIOTISM

is what the flag stands for!

We support our country. Citizens of the United States have a love for their country and what it represents.

ROCK USA

Core Democratic Va

RULE OF LAW

Laws are made for the good of everyone. Both the government and the people of the nation must obey all laws.

REPRESENTATIVE GOVERNMENT

Citizens elect others to represent them and act for them in government.

It's importANT to VOTE!

CHECKS AND BALANCES

No branch of government can have more power than the other. One branch checks or balances the power of the other branches so that no branch is stronger or more powerful than another.

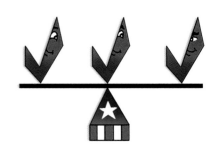

SEPARATION OF POWERS

EXECUTIVE

LEGISLATIVE

JUDICIAL

Both the state and national governments are divided into three branches—the legislative, which makes laws; the executive, which carries out the laws; and the judicial, which interprets the laws.

Legislative - House of Representatives and Senate

Executive - The President or Governor and their cabinet members

Judicial - Supreme Court and lower courts

CONSTITUTIONAL PRINCIPLES •

 ⭐ **INDIVIDUAL RIGHTS**

All people have certain basic rights. These include life, liberty, privacy and the pursuit of happiness. It is the duty of the government to protect these rights.

⭐ **FREEDOM OF RELIGION**

Citizens have the freedom to choose whatever religion they want to follow, or to follow no religion.

CIVILIAN CONTROL OF THE MILITARY

⭐ Civilian (non-military) people should be in charge of the military by electing leaders to speak for them in government.

It works for *me* and for *EVERY* American!

⭐ **FEDERALISM**

The state and national governments share power and responsibilities. This keeps the national government from having complete power.

 ☆

The flag is a symbol for our country. It stands for our nation's basic ideas and principles. Our flag, sometimes called the *"Stars and Stripes"* and *"Old Glory,"* symbolizes the union of 50 states and over 280 million people into one *Great Country*... the United States of America. It stands for people... millions of Americans, past and present, who have worked and fought to preserve our freedom and way of life.

It's *YOUR FLAG*... it stands for *your country* "...conceived in liberty and dedicated to the proposition that all men and women are created equal."

TREAT IT WITH THE ESTEEM AND RESPECT IT DESERVES.

The United States "Flag Code" was adopted in 1923.

DISPLAYING THE FLAG

Half mast

During the day -
On any day when the weather is good, the flag can be displayed outside from sunrise to sunset on buildings and stationary poles. The flag can be displayed on bad-weather days if an all-weather flag is used.

Don't let the flag touch the ground.
Fold it as it comes down, before completely detaching it from *halyard*. The flag is usually lowered at night. If a patriotic effect is desired, the flag may be displayed 24 hours a day (if properly illuminated during darkness).

As a sign of mourning,
display the flag at half mast by hoisting to peak and then lowering to half mast. On Memorial Day fly at half mast until noon; then raise to peak until sunset. If your flag is on an *outrigger flagpole* or mounted on a wall and cannot be flown at half mast, it is appropriate to drape a purple and black mourning ribbon across the flag.

CARE OF FLAG

To Fold: Fold flag in fourths, lengthwise. Then make successive diagonal folds, ending with union outside (the union is the blue part of the flag with stars). Unless using an all-weather flag, don't expose it to bad weather. Dispose of an old flag the approved way—"...destroy it in a dignified way, preferably by burning."

Contact your local American Legion for dates of dignified burning ceremonies

STEP 1   STEP 2   STEP 3

ur Flag!

DISPLAYING THE FLAG continued.

Crossed On Wall
U.S. flag outside, on observers' left.

Flat On Wall
Union always on top, to observers' left.

On Same Staff
U.S. flag at peak, above any other flags.

Grouped
U.S. flag in center, or at highest point.

Grouped...
.S. flag goes to its own right, is hoisted first. ags of different nations flown at same height.

Over A Street...
Flag vertical; union faces north (on east-west streets) or east (on north-south streets).

On Speaker's Platform
Flag above and behind speaker or on STAFF to his/her right.

How to PLEDGE ALLEGIANCE *to our flag*

"I pledge allegiance to the flag of the United States of America and to the Republic for which it stands, one nation under God, indivisible, with liberty and justice for all."

- Head bare
  (women leave hats on; people in uniform leave hats on and give hand salute)
- Right hand over heart
- Standing at attention

In Audience...
In front of audience nd to speaker's right hen facing audience.

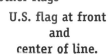

In Procession with other flags

U.S. flag to marchers' right (observers' left).

U.S. flag at front and center of line.

When folded properly the flag looks like this...

WHAT THE COLORS MEAN

RED - symbolizes HARDINESS and VALOR
WHITE - symbolizes PURITY and INNOCENCE
BLUE - symbolizes VIGILANCE and JUSTICE

STEP 4   **START FOLD HERE**

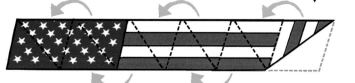

God Bless America
Irving Berlin
(1888-1989)
Used by Permission.

God bless America,
Land that I love,
Stand beside her and guide her
Through the night with a light from above.
From the mountains, to the prairies,
To the oceans white with foam,
God bless America,
My home sweet home.

You're a Grand Old Flag
George M. Cohan
(1878-1942)

You're a grand old flag,
You're a high-flying flag,
And forever in peace may you wave
You're the emblem of
The land I love.
The home of the free and the brave
Ev'ry heart beats true
'Neath the Red, White and Blue
Where there's never a boast or brag
Should auld acquaintance be forgot
Keep your eye on the grand old flag

The Star-Spangled Banner
Francis Scott Key
(1779-1843)

O, say can you see by the dawn's
early light,
What so proudly we hailed at the
twilight's last gleaming?
Whose broad stripes and bright stars,
Through the perilous fight
O'er the ramparts we watched were
so gallantly streaming?
And the rocket's red glare, the
bombs bursting in air,
Gave proof through the night that
our flag was still there.
O, say, does that star-spangled
banner yet wave
O'er the land of the free and the
home of the brave?

I ★ White and Blue !

God Bless the U.S.A.
Lee Greenwood
(1942-present)
Used by Permission.

If tomorrow all the things were gone
I'd worked for all my life,
And I had to start again
with just my children and my wife,
I'd thank my lucky stars
to be living here today,
'Cause the flag still stands for freedom
and they can't take that away.

And I'm proud to be an American
where at least I know I'm free,
And I won't forget the men who died
who gave that right to me,
And I gladly stand up next to you
and defend her still today,
'Cause there ain't no doubt I love this land
God Bless the U.S.A.

From the lakes of Minnesota
to the hills of Tennessee,
Across the plains of Texas
from sea to shining sea.
From Detroit down to Houston
and New York to L.A.,
There's pride in every American heart
and it's time we stand and say:

That I'm proud to be an American
where at least I know I'm free,
And I won't forget the men who died
who gave that right to me,
And I gladly stand up next to you
and defend her still today,
'Cause there ain't no doubt I love this land
God Bless the U.S.A.

America
Samuel Francis Smith
(1808-1895)

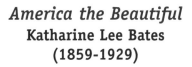

My country, 'tis of thee,
Sweet land of liberty,
Of thee I sing.
Land where my fathers died,
Land of the Pilgrim's pride,
From every mountainside
Let freedom ring!

America the Beautiful
Katharine Lee Bates
(1859-1929)

O beautiful for spacious skies,
For amber waves of grain,
For purple mountain majesties
Above the fruited plain!
America! America!
God shed his grace on thee
And crown thy good with
    brotherhood
From sea to shining sea!

This Land Is Your Land
Woodie Guthrie
(1912-1967)
Used by Permission.

This land is your land,
This land is my land,
From California
To the New York island,
From the redwood forest,
To the Gulf Stream waters,
This land was made for you and me.

As I was walking a ribbon of highway,
I saw above me an endless skyway,
I saw below me a golden valley.
This land was made for you and me.

About the Author and Illustrator

Edna Cucksey Stephens...

is the co-author of *Looking At Animals with Mr. Etch A Sketch®*, the award-winning *Michigan L.A.P.'s™ Program*, a Michigan history and natural resources curriculum, the Michigan Department of Natural Resources' *Outdoor Explorers Club* newsletter, children's stories and other educational materials. She taught elementary school for twenty-six years in Lake Orion, Michigan. Edna lives with her husband, Mark, in Clarkston, Michigan. They have two grown children, Scot and Cari.

Mark J. Herrick...

is the illustrator of the *Michigan L.A.P.'s™ Program*, the Michigan Department of Natural Resources' *Outdoor Explorers Club* newsletter, the award-winning *Buck Wilder's Small Twig Hiking and Camping Guide* and *Buck Wilder's Small Fry Fishing Guide*. In 2000, Mark was chosen to create the White House Easter Egg for Michigan and a piece of his artwork traveled to the Space Station Mir with Astronaut Jerry Linenger. Mark lives in Holly, Michigan.

Visit us at:
www.ROCKUSA.net

American Dream